OPEN SEASON™

THE MIGHTY GRIZZLY

HarperCollins®, 📖®, and HarperKidsEntertainment™
are trademarks of HarperCollins Publishers.

For information address HarperCollins Children's Books, a division of HarperCollins Publishers,
1350 Avenue of the Americas, New York, NY 10019.
Book design by John Sazaklis
www.harpercollinschildrens.com
Library of Congress catalog card number: 2006926602
ISBN-10: 0-06-084607-0 — ISBN-13: 978-0-06-084607-7
❖
First Edition

THE MIGHTY GRIZZLY

Adapted by Jasmine Jones

HarperKidsEntertainment
A Imprint of HarperCollinsPublishers

Chapter One

"Behold, the mighty grizzly!" Ranger Beth said as she stood beside Boog, a giant grizzly bear. The crowd at the amphitheater loved him, and they exploded with applause as Boog rode around the stage on a tiny unicycle. Boog, loving the attention, flashed a huge grin to the audience.

"We rocked the house, didn't we, Boog?" Ranger Beth said to the giant grizzly bear beside her as they walked through the amphitheater's backstage door.

Boog grunted in agreement. He was huge, with

long teeth and sharp claws. But Beth had raised him. Now Boog performed in Timberline's Wildlife Show. On the outside, he was a grizzly bear, but on the inside, he was more like a teddy bear.

"They were eating out of our hands!" Beth said excitedly. But suddenly the smile vanished from Beth's face. Parked next to her jeep was a familiar truck. A one-horned deer was strapped to the hood. The other horn was just a broken stump. "That's Shaw's truck!" Beth fumed. "You wait here, Boog."

Boog climbed into the back of the jeep while Beth went into the Fish and Game office to talk to the truck's owner. There were still three days left before open season, but Shaw had obviously started hunting

early. Beth was going to give him a piece of her mind.

Yawning, Boog settled down into the back of the jeep. But a weird noise jolted him awake. It sounded like it had come from the deer.

Leaning over the side of the jeep, Boog poked at the deer with a stick.

One eye popped open. "Aaaaahh!" cried the deer, whose name was Elliot.

"Aaaaahh!" shouted Boog. He jumped back in fear.

"Am I dead?" Elliot asked.

"Not yet," Boog said.

Elliot looked around. "Untie me?" he begged. "Please? I don't want to be mounted on a wall!"

Boog shook his head. "Ain't gonna be able to do it."

Just then, Beth walked out of the office. "Boog, come on," she said. "Let's get out of here."

"Come on . . ." Elliot whispered to the bear once Beth had turned her back. "Pleasepleaseplease!"

Boog rolled his eyes and sighed. Finally, he reached over and slashed at Elliot's ropes, freeing him. "Hey, go on, now," Boog said as the jeep started to pull away. "Scamper back to the woods, little buddy."

"Buddy?" Elliot repeated as Boog disappeared. "He called me 'buddy'!"

Just then, Shaw burst out of the Fish and Game office. He had seen Boog untie Elliot from the office window. "My buck!" he screeched.

Shaw took aim at Elliot as he darted away, but Sheriff Gordy stopped him. He reached out and pushed Shaw's rifle down.

"Shaw, no shooting in town!" Gordy said.

"But, but Gordy," Shaw sputtered, "that bear leaned over and untied my buck!"

Gordy laughed. "Shaw, you've been living in the woods too long."

Shaw snarled. He knew what he'd seen. And he was determined to get even.

"Good night, big guy!" Beth said softly to Boog. It was nighttime and Boog had just snuggled in bed with his

tiny blue teddy bear backpack, Dinkelman.

Beth sang Boog the special lullaby that always helped him drift off to sleep. Once his eyes were closed, she tucked a blanket over him and closed the door to the garage. "Good night, Boog," she whispered again.

Ponk!

A strange noise startled Boog. He looked up.

Ponk! Ponk!

Boog frowned. Someone was tossing rabbits at his window! "Who's there?" Boog called.

Outside, Elliot tossed another rabbit at the window. "Hey, buddy!" he said, shoving his head in the window. "It's me, Elliot! I'm bustin' you out of here!"

Scrambling into the garage, Elliot started shoving Boog toward the door. "Let's book it before the warden makes her rounds."

Boog didn't budge. "Nah, nah, cornflake, you got it all twisted," he explained. "This is my home."

Elliot blinked in surprise. He looked around the garage. It was half empty. The other half was crammed with junk—empty bottles, rusty tools, a TV.

"Sweet!" Elliot said. He started to explore. "So soft," he said as he jumped up and down on Boog's bed. In a flash, he darted into the bathroom and started unrolling the toilet paper.

"Whoa! What are you doing in there?" Boog cried.

Elliot zipped around the garage. "Ooh, who's this little guy?" he asked, picking up Boog's teddy bear.

"Dinkelman!" Boog cried.

Elliot laughed. "Is Dinkelman your . . . doll?" The deer looked at Boog's food bowl and bed. "Oh! I get it!" he said. "You're like a pet!"

"I ain't nobody's pet," Boog huffed. "I come and go as I please."

Elliot opened the garage door. "Well, then . . . let's go!"

Chapter Two

After smelling the heavenly scent of Elliot's chocolate bar, Boog wanted a candy bar of his own. Elliot promised him that the PuniMart, the town convenience store, held all the chocolate bars he could ever imagine eating. And so Boog and Elliot snuck down to the PuniMart, looking for more candy. When they arrived, they saw shelves filled with candy as far as the eye could see! Eager to get in, Elliot stole a shopping cart and crashed it through the front door. Boog and Elliot ran through the store, gobbling up chips,

soft drinks, and sweets. All the sugar made the two animals crazy. They made such a mess that someone called Sheriff Gordy.

"Freeze!" Gordy shouted.

"Behold, the mighty grizzly!" Boog shouted as he danced around the PuniMart as Elliot escaped out the back door.

Gordy drove Boog home in the back of his sheriff's van.

Beth was waiting outside as they pulled up. "You're in big trouble, mister," she told Boog angrily. "Straight to bed. Now!"

Gordy looked at Beth as Boog stumbled toward the garage. "What if he had hurt someone?" Gordy asked. "It's time you put him out in the woods where he belongs—"

"No, no, no," Beth interrupted. "He's not ready to go."

"Beth, you're not his mother," Gordy said gently. "The longer you wait, the harder it's going to be for him to learn to live in the woods. And the harder it's going to be for you to let him go."

Beth's shoulders slumped. Gordy was right, and she knew it. "But what about hunting season?" she asked.

"Take him above the falls," Gordy suggested. "He'll be safe there."

The fading orange sunlight glowed over the Sawtooth Mountains as Beth piloted the helicopter above the forest. In a huge net beneath the helicopter, Boog was sleeping, snuggled tightly in a sack with Dinkelman. Beth flew high into the mountains, over the meadows and a waterfall, where Boog would be safe from the hunters.

Finally, Beth lowered the net gently and landed the helicopter. Sighing, she untied Boog. "You're gonna be . . . you're gonna be fine," she whispered to the sleeping bear as she placed Dinkelman under his chin. She pulled the bag around him, tucking both of them in. "I'm going to miss you, big guy." Beth hugged Boog for a long time. Then she climbed into the helicopter and took off into the starry night sky.

Chapter Three

The sun rose, casting a golden glow over the lush green meadow where Boog lay sleeping. Birds chirped, squirrels chattered—and Boog snored.

Buzzz! A bee floated by, snapping Boog awake.

"Aaahhh!" he screamed as he stared at the wilderness around him. "Where's home? It's gone! Someone stole it!"

"Hey, could you keep it down?" Elliot asked as he popped his head out of Boog's bag. Beth had caught him and released him into the wilderness, too. "I'm trying to sleep here." Elliot yawned. Furious, Boog grabbed Elliot by one horn and pulled him out of the bag. "My garage is missing!" Boog shouted. "My life is missing! And it's all your fault!" Boog tossed Elliot into the air and flung him over his shoulder. "Think, Boog," the bear commanded himself. "She's mad, but you can fix this."

When Elliot landed, his one good antler got stuck in the ground. "Boog!" Elliot cried as he struggled to free himself. "You can't just go wandering around out here. You don't know where you're going."

"I'm going home," Boog announced.

"Wait, Boog! I know where Timberline is," Elliot lied. "I can get you back!"

Boog unzipped Dinkelman and pulled out two long straps. Then he shouldered his teddy bear backpack. "Thank you, but no thank you." Boog stormed off while Elliot wrestled with his antler, which was still stuck in the ground.

"Timberline has got to be around here somewhere," Boog muttered to himself.

Stomp, stomp, stomp.

"Well, that was quick," Elliot said as Boog appeared behind him. Boog had wound up right back where he started!

Grumbling, Boog stomped back into the forest.

Stomp, stomp, stomp.

"Oh!" Boog cried as he came face-to-face with Elliot—who was still stuck. He thundered off again, looking for Timberline.

"Boog, is that you?" Elliot asked as Boog tramped by again.

Exhausted, Boog collapsed over a log. "Okay," he said, breathing heavily, "I gotta get the lay of the land. Somehow, if I can get up high enough, then . . ." He looked up at a towering pine tree. "All right," he said to himself. "I can do this." Boog reached for the tree.

"Oi!" bellowed a voice. "This is McSquizzy's turf. Nobody messes with McSquizzy, 'cause that's me!" Suddenly, a squirrel with bristling eyebrows and a twitchy tail appeared before Boog and Elliot. Aside from being an overprotective squirrel, he was also the leader of the Furry Tail Clan.

"What?" Boog looked up into the face of a very fuzzy, very fierce squirrel.

"Touch a needle on this tree and I'll give you such a doin'!" McSquizzy warned.

"Yeah?" Boog snickered. "You and what army?"

McSquizzy let out a shrill whistle, and in a flash the tree was thick with an army of squirrels. "Oi!" they all called.

"Mess not with the Furry Tail Clan," McSquizzy trilled. "Guardians of the Pine!"

"Keep your tree," Boog grumbled. "I'll find another one." The bear turned his back on the squirrels and started walking away.

"Look!" McSquizzy cried, catching sight of Boog's Dinkelman backpack. "He's got a wee freakish twin growin' out of his back!"

The squirrels chattered with laughter.

Scowling, Boog walked over to another tree. "This one'll work. . . ."

Bonk!

"Ouch!" Boog cried. McSquizzy had just knocked him on the head with an acorn.

"That was a warning, all right?" McSquizzy flicked his tail.

"Oi!" the Furry Tail Clan agreed.

"What?" Boog demanded angrily. "This is a different tree!"

"They're all my trees!" McSquizzy announced. "I suggest you turn around and head right back from whence you came."

"That's what I'm trying to do," Boog explained. "So just show me the way to town, and I'll be out of here."

All of the squirrels pointed in different directions. Then they cracked up laughing.

"That's it!" Boog shouted. "You're asking for a whoopin'!" He lunged toward the tree trunk.

"Ready?" McSquizzy called. "Fire!"

A storm of acorns rained down on Boog.

It looked like he was going to have to find another way back to Timberline.

Chapter Four

"**H**ey, Boog, look!" Elliot cried as the bear stumbled back into the clearing. The deer was balancing upside down on his antler. "No hands!"

Ignoring him, Boog collapsed on the ground. Then he shook the acorns out of his fur. "All right," he said angrily. "Where's town?" He yanked Elliot out of the ground.

"Okay, okay," Elliot said. "You got it pretty good in Timberline, right?"

Boog shrugged. "Yeah, so—"

"I want in, Boog!" Elliot cried. "I'll take you to town, but when we get there, we're partners. Deal?"

"What?" Boog dropped Elliot. "That ain't never gonna happen! Don't you have a herd to get back to?"

"My herd . . . my herd will understand," Elliot lied. "They want the best for me."

"Forget it," Boog snapped.

"Better start moving, then," Elliot said, "'cause open season starts in a few days. Maybe one of those hunters can give you a ride back on the hood of their truck."

"Hunters!" Boog thought for a moment. He remembered Shaw and how angry he was that Boog had set Elliot free. Shaw would love to hunt down a big bear like Boog. "Dang. Okay, okay, " Boog said.

"So we have a deal, then?" Elliot asked excitedly. "Okay, let me hear you say it." He spat on his hoof and held it out. "Partners?"

"I . . . guess . . . we can be . . . partners," Boog mumbled.

"P . . . p . . . partners?" Elliot teased.

Boog sighed. "Partners," he said, taking Elliot's hoof in his paw.

"Okeydokey!" Elliot began to trot off. "This way!'"

Elliot set off with his new friend, excited to show Boog the forest.

"Okay, Forest 101," Elliot explained as he led Boog in and out of the trees.

"Ah . . . ah . . . ah-choo!" Boog sniffled miserably. He was starting to think that he might be allergic to the wilderness.

"These big wood stick things are called trees," Elliot went on. He bounded up a steep slope. "The big rocks are called mountains, and the little rocks are their babies."

Boog struggled after him. He was so tired that his arms started to wobble. "No jelly arm . . ." he told himself. "No jelly arm . . ." The big bear slipped. "Elliot!" he screeched, clinging to the side of the mountain with one paw.

Boog lost his grip and slid down the mountainside. "Oof! Agh! Ugh!" He dropped down on a tree and crashed from branch to branch, landing on an outstretched limb. His butt was dangling only two feet above the ground.

"Yeah, okay," Boog said in relief as he eased himself off of the branch. "I got it. Nice and easy."

Just then, a porcupine waddled under the tree to sniff a flower.

Boog dropped—right onto the porcupine.

"Aiiieee!"

"Just rip it off fast," Boog told Elliot as he bent over with his butt in the air.

"Hold still!" Elliot commanded. "Just be calm, this might pinch a little," he told the porcupine.

The porcupine gave him a thumbs-up.

With a quick motion, Elliot ripped the porcupine off of Boog's butt!

Boog let out a very loud howl as Elliot set the porcupine gently on the ground and gave him a little shove. "Okay," Elliot said, "scamper back to the woods, little buddy."

Elliot and Boog turned to leave. Boog was still rubbing his rump.

The porcupine trotted after them. "Buddee . . ." he said, gazing after Elliot.

Chapter Five

After a while, Boog and Elliot came upon a group of beavers working on a dam in a river.

"Hey, hey, guys!" the boss beaver—whose name was Reilly—called. "Check it out!" He pointed to Boog. "The largest omnivore in North America, the mighty grizzly."

The other beavers murmured in admiration.

Elliot stopped in his tracks. "And he's a good dancer," the deer added proudly. "We're gonna be in a show."

The beavers cracked up—Boog was obviously not a wild bear.

Embarrassed by the beavers' teasing, Boog grabbed Elliot by his antler and yanked him away from the dam. "Listen, simple," snapped the bear. "We are not we! It's just me! And we ain't doing no show!"

"*Diva*," Elliot muttered under his breath. He

sighed. "I understand what's going on here—you're a little crabby because you're hungry."

"I . . . uh . . . no . . ." Boog shook his head.

"Hmmm?" Elliot widened his eyes. "I think yes."

Boog's eyes filled with tears. "I'm starving," he admitted.

Elliot handed him a pinecone. "Here," he said, "try this."

"I can't eat that." Boog curled his lip.

"Picky, picky, picky!" Elliot rolled his eyes. "Well, what do bears eat?"

Boog thought for a moment. Usually, he ate whatever Beth fed him. But wild bears must eat something. "Umm . . . ah . . ." He scratched his head. Suddenly, it came to him. "Fish! Bears eat fish!"

Boog looked down at the rushing water, which was thick with swimming salmon. "All right, fishies," Boog called, "give it up for Boog!"

Three giant silver salmon jumped gracefully out of the water.

"Hi-ya!" they screeched, slapping the bear silly with their tails.

Boog fell into the water with a splash. He obviously had no idea how to fish.

This wasn't exactly the delicious meal he'd had in mind.

Boog stormed deeper into the wilderness, with Elliot right behind him.

Suddenly, Elliot caught sight of the most beautiful doe in the forest. She had large eyes, as blue as a summer sky. "Giselle!" Elliot cried.

Ignoring him, Boog went on ahead and came upon another stream. "The woods are no place for a bear," he grumbled as two ducks paddled by. His face brightened. "Ducks!"

Boog peeked over his shoulder. Elliot was busy trying to tie a tree branch to the stump where his one antler had broken off. Now was Boog's chance to lose the deer. "Quick!" he said to the ducks. "I'm looking for town. Could one of you guys fly up high to see it, then show me the way?"

Deni, the smaller duck, panicked. "Fly!" he screeched. "Fly!"

"Quiet!" Boog said, shushing the excitable duck. "He'll hear you!"

But Elliot was busy. He wanted to talk to the beautiful doe. *"Pst!"* Elliot whispered. "Giselle!"

Giselle smiled. "Elliot!" Suddenly, her voice turned serious. "You better get out of here," she said in a whisper. "You remember what happened the last time you talked to me."

Elliot's heart started to pound. "Oh," he said nervously. "Is Ian around?"

Just then, a giant buck appeared through the high grass of the meadow, followed by the rest of the herd. "Hello, Smelliot," Ian said. "Ha! I called him Smelliot!"

The rest of the herd cracked up.

The huge buck towered over Elliot. "I told you to leave the herd and never, ever come back!"

"I'm not back!" Elliot insisted. "Me and my best buddy are heading to town." He patted Ian on the chest.

"Off the upholstery!" Ian shouted, head-butting Elliot with his giant antlers.

"Aiiiieee!" Elliot sailed into the air.

Boog heard the scream. "What now?" he said to himself as he took off running. The bear charged into the circle of deer just as Elliot landed with a crunch at Ian's feet. Boog let out a roar.

"Bear!" Ian screamed. The whole herd took a step back as Boog leaned over to help his friend.

"Elliot," Boog said, "are you all right?"

One of the deer noticed Boog's Dinkelman backpack and plucked it with his teeth. "Hey, Ian!" the deer called. "Get a load of this!"

"Cut it out!" Boog cried, as he grabbed it back.

"Oh, I've heard of you," Ian said slowly. He wasn't afraid of Boog anymore. "You're that bear that got his butt thumped by a squirrel. Ha! Ha!"

"Boog," Elliot said, tugging at the bear's arm, "let's go."

Elliot and Boog turned to leave, but Ian blocked their way. "You two are perfect for each other," he taunted. "You're a loser . . ." Ian nodded to Elliot. Then he turned to Boog. ". . . and you're a loser . . . er!"

Ian and the herd bounded away. Giselle waited a moment. "Bye, Elliot," she said softly.

Elliot looked at her sadly. "Yeah," he said. "See ya."

"See you later, backpack boy!" Ian shouted back at Boog.

Boog waited until the herd couldn't hear him anymore, then shouted, "That's right, fool! You better run!"

"Yeah!" Elliot chimed in. "One more word and I was gonna rack him."

Boog patted Elliot on the back. "That's right!"

The two friends nodded. But despite the brave front, deep down inside both Elliot and Boog were happy the herd had left. Ian and the herd really had a way with their antlers!

Chapter Six

Boog and Elliot continued walking in the forest until they came upon some tall grass to make beds for the evening.

"That was, uh, Ian's girl you were trying to talk to, wasn't it?" Boog said as he plopped down into the grass.

Elliot nodded. "Ian's right," he said with a sigh. "I'm a loser."

"No, you're not a loser," Boog said.

"Trust me." Elliot pointed to the stump on his head where his antler used to be. "The day I met you, Ian kicked me out of the herd, I lost my antler, and I got run over and tied to the hood of a truck. What do you call that?"

Boog thought for a moment. "A loser," he admitted.

Elliot slumped.

"But check this out," Boog said, getting to his feet. "I look like a bear. I talk like a bear. But I can't fish and I can't climb a tree."

"Well, at least you've got a home." Elliot sounded miserable.

Boog sighed. He missed Beth and his bed. He pulled off Dinkelman and fluffed him like a pillow. "Yeah," he said. "I hope so." Boog thought about home. "To be back in my own soft bed! Eight square meals a day . . . plus snacks. Beth tucking me in every night. It's like heaven to me." The bear let out a large, contented sigh.

Looking up, Boog noticed that Elliot was watching him. He looked about as sad as a deer can look.

"You know . . . uh . . ." Boog said slowly, "when we get back home tomorrow, I'm going to make things right with Beth." He let out a huge yawn. "And maybe—just maybe—we can find a place for you in the garage with me!"

Elliot's eyes lit up. "Sweet!" Elliot settled down, imagining himself having a home. "I'm sleeping in the garage," he sang quietly to himself. "I'm sleeping in the garage. . . ."

"Hey, Elliot, do me a favor, will ya?" Boog asked. "Will you sing me a lullaby?"

"Sure, I'll give it a shot," Elliot responded.

Elliot started out with hesitation. "Uh, once there was a magical elf who lived in a rainbow tree. He lived downstairs from a flatulent dwarf who was constantly having to pee. . . ."

Elliot continued singing, but halfway through the first verse, Boog was fast asleep.

The next morning, Boog and Elliot woke up early and started on their way toward Timberline.

"I had some thoughts on the show," Elliot announced as the two tramped through the forest. He was carrying Dinkelman.

"Whoa!" Boog cried. "*My* show?"

"The lady in the shorts has got to go," Elliot declared as he and Boog passed a small stream. "It's gotta be fresh and new; I want some jazz."

"Whoa, whoa, whoa!" Boog said angrily. "That's my show. The people come out there to see me, a grizzly bear!"

"Oh, I see!" Elliot cried, hurt. "You get to have the career while I stay home and look after Dinkelman!"

He threw the teddy on the ground and leaned against a tree.

"Oi!"

It was McSquizzy again.

Elliot nearly fell over under an avalanche of nuts. Sighing, Boog picked up Dinkelman.

"Buddee . . ." said a voice.

That voice—it almost sounded like the porcupine he had accidentally sat on. But when Boog looked around, nobody was there. But he did see something familiar—a beaver dam!

"Elliot!" Boog cried. "Aren't those the same beavers?"

"No." Elliot sniffed, as though that was the most ridiculous thing he had ever heard. "All beavers look alike."

"Hey! Tiny Dancer!" Reilly shouted as the other beavers behind him began to laugh and dance. "Let's see some moves!" Reilly called.

"Elliot!" Boog bellowed. "This is the same dam! We've been going in circles!"

Elliot gulped. "Circle," he whispered. "One time around . . ."

"Argh!" Boog roared. "You don't even know where we're going!"

Ka-blam!

Boog and Elliot dropped to the ground as a gun-shot exploded the tree behind them. It was Shaw!

"Wahoo!" Shaw shouted, dancing for joy. "Got 'em!"

"What was that?" Boog cried, jumping to his feet.

"Hunters?" hollered one of the beavers. "What's a hunter doing here? Open season hasn't started yet!" he screamed. The beavers were worried about other hunters taking aim, so they quickly dove into the lake.

"Boog!" Elliot shouted. "We gotta hide!"

"I'm out of here," Boog said. He clutched Dinkelman to his chest and bolted across the dam.

"Tubby!" Reilly called. "Stop! This ain't a load-bearing structure!"

Snap!

A branch broke and Boog dropped between the logs. Tiny leaks spurted out down the face of the dam.

"Oh," Elliot said to himself, "that's bad."

The dam collapsed with a giant *whoosh!*

"Aaaaahh!" Boog and Elliot cried as they were swept downstream by the water.

A huge wave washed them down the mountainside into the meadow, picking up logs and animals as it rushed along. The water pulled Dinkelman away from Boog and even swept Shaw's truck down the riverbed, which meant that the water wasn't their only problem. . . .

"Where are we going to hide?" asked Maria the skunk.

"Guys, it's not his fault," Elliot said, putting a hoof on his friend's arm.

"You're right, Elliot . . ." Boog snapped, pulling his arm away from Elliot. "It's your fault! If it weren't for you, none of this would have ever happened. You said you knew the way back! But you lied." Elliot didn't know what to say, because Boog was right—he really didn't know the way home.

"I thought if you hung out with me, you'd like me," Elliot admitted.

"I'm better off alone," Boog announced.

Thunder rolled as dark clouds appeared on the horizon.

"What about us?" asked the porcupine.

"There is no *us*!" Boog shouted. "You're not my problem. And you," he added, as he pointed to Elliot, "we're done."

As night began to descend on the valley, it started to rain, further drenching the animals.

Boog stormed off, leaving Elliot—leaving everyone—behind.

Chapter Seven

"**T**rees, bushes, rain . . ." Boog grumbled as he stomped through the dark, wet forest. Above him, the rain pitter-pattered against the leaves. "Stupid nature!" He hurried through the darkness and tripped. Boog looked down. Two yellow lines?

Headlights shone in his eyes as trucks barreled up the road. Boog panicked as he saw the hunters driving up to the campgrounds. Open season was only a few hours away! Boog retreated to the bushes to hide. Once the trucks had disappeared, Boog tiptoed to the middle of the road. In the other direction, silver lights twinkled: Timberline. Home.

Pausing, Boog looked back toward the trucks. He could still see them in the distance. "Elliot," Boog said quietly to himself. He knew that his friend was in danger.

All of the animals were in danger.

Even though he wanted to see Beth more than anything, there was no way Boog could go back to his cozy little home without trying to help.

When the animals saw the trucks, they tried to hide themselves. All of the animals, that is, except for one. Elliot was shuffling miserably into the clearing, singing sadly to himself. Giselle saw him and tried to warn him. "Elliot," she whispered, "you've got to hide! The hunters are here."

Elliot sighed as he halfheartedly tried to hide behind a rotten tree, but his tail stuck out. All he could do was keep singing his sad little song.

"Oh, no," Reilly said nervously from under a bush, "he's going to give us away."

But just then, someone ripped Elliot from the tree!

"All right, bring it, bring it!" Elliot shouted, hanging upside down. He swung out, throwing punches wildly, eyes closed.

Then he heard a familiar laugh.

"Boog?" Elliot asked, opening one eye.

Boog grinned. "Hey, buddy!"

"What are you doing back here?" Elliot asked.

"Come on," Boog said. "I couldn't go home without my partner."

Elliot looked at Boog sideways. He wasn't sure he wanted a partner anymore.

"C'mon," Boog urged. "Let me hear you say it—" He dropped his voice to a whisper: "Partners."

"I guess we can be partners," Elliot mumbled.

Boog cupped one ear. "Sorry, I can't hear you."

"I said, 'I guess we can be partners,'" Elliot said, grudgingly.

"P . . . p . . . p . . ." Boog teased.

"Partners!" the two friends said together as they laughed.

Boog dropped Elliot, who popped right back onto his feet. "Okeydokey!" he cried, heading off in the wrong direction. "This way!"

Boog grabbed his friend by the antler and turned

him around. "This way."

"Right," Elliot agreed. "Maybe you'd better lead."

"Yeah . . ." Boog looked around nervously. "Let's get back to the garage, where it's safe."

Reilly's head popped up from behind a rock. "Safe?" he said.

"Safe?" Giselle said, popping out of a bush.

Rabbits and skunks popped up. "Safe?" they all said.

Elliot and Boog were sneaking from tree to tree, as the forest was now full of hunters. They were camping out in anticipation of open season's arrival in just a few short hours.

"Huh?" Elliot said when he noticed something behind him. "Hey, Boog," he whispered. "How many animals can fit in the garage?"

"How many what?" Boog repeated. Then he turned and looked back. "Whoa!"

They were being followed by almost every animal in the forest.

"Hi, Boog!" the animals shouted.

Boog stood nervously in front of the crowd. "So . . ." he said uncomfortably. "Where you all headed?"

"To the safe place," Giselle said.

"This Land of Garage," Ian added.

"With buddee!" the porcupine chimed in, gazing at Elliot.

"C'mon," Reilly shouted, "you owe us, Tiny!"

The animals murmured their agreement.

"Oh, yeah, um . . ." Boog shuffled his feet. "Sorry about your dam . . ." he said to the beavers. "And how I messed y'all up," he added to the other animals. "My bad."

"Please!" Ian begged. "I'm too pretty to die!"

Boog looked at the animals, picturing them all squashed into the tiny garage.

"No!" he yelled. "That would never work!"

The animals ran toward him. "Why not?" shouted Reilly.

"Come on!" cried the skunk.

"Pleeeease," begged the porcupine.

"Now wait! Let me think!" Boog said, backing away from them.

But when he turned around, he stopped dead in his tracks.

His way home was blocked—by dozens of flickering campfires. The forest was full of hunters. The animals were trapped!

"Dang," Boog said quietly. "Nobody's going home tonight."

"There's so many of them," said Reilly.

"That's it, then," Giselle said.

"No more me," cried the porcupine sadly.

Elliot's eyes were wide. "I guess I'm going to be mounted on a wall."

Boog looked down at his friend's frightened face, then back at the campfires. "No you won't," Boog said. "I ain't going without a fight!" He looked at the surprised animals. "If there's one thing you all have taught me—the woods is a messed-up, dangerous place . . . and y'all are crazy." The bear's belly shook as he laughed. "You've been kicking *my* butt for the last two days."

The animals looked at each other, then started to giggle.

"I say we do to them what you've been doing to me!" Boog said. "Let's give our guests the full outdoor experience."

"Yeah!" the animals shouted.

A voice boomed from a branch above. "Is this a private fight?" McSquizzy called. "Or can anyone join? Because McSquizzy wants in!"

An army of squirrels popped out of the tree.

"Oi!" shouted the Furry Tail Clan.

There was no doubt—the battle was *on*. The animals snuck away to prepare.

Chapter Eight

Later that night, Elliot led the other animals in a raid on a nearby campsite. They spotted an Airstream trailer that looked deserted. They gathered supplies they would need for their battle with the hunters. Reilly grabbed a chain saw, McSquizzy took a propane tank, and the porcupine ran off with marshmallows stuck to his quills.

"Grr!"

Elliot and Boog stopped in their tracks. A dachshund in a blue sweater was growling at them.

"It's a pet!" the porcupine cried.

Reilly snarled, "He's gonna blow our cover!"

But the wiener dog didn't bark. Instead, he ripped off his sweater. "I've been living a lie! Please take me with you!" Mr. Weenie begged.

Naturally, the animals agreed—they needed all the help they could get.

By the following morning—the first day of open season—everything was ready. The hunters, dressed in dark camouflage, snuck silently through the trees.

Boog sent up the signal, and in a moment, a squadron of ducks—led by Deni and Serge—flew over the forest. Each duck carried a skunk.

"All right, ladies!" called Maria the skunk. "Let her rip!"

The skunks blanketed the forest in a stinky smog of skunk spray! The hunters staggered, choking and gasping in the fumes.

Boog handed out rabbits for the beavers to use as gas masks—then the beavers charged the hunters.

"My pants!" cried a hunter as Reilly and his crew ran through the grass grabbing boxer shorts and tighty whities.

"Chaaarge!" Elliot cried as he rode Ian like a giant horse into the skunk-fogged meadow. The rest of the herd galloped behind.

55

"It's a stampede!" shouted a scared hunter.

"All right!" Boog commanded his troops. "Show me your grr! face!"

"Grr!" growled the porcupine, who wore a colander as a battle helmet.

"Grr!" snarled the rabbits, pulling out plastic forks, knives, and spoons.

toward the hunters just as Boog and his group crashed into them from the other side.

With a forceful sneeze, the porcupine sent dozens of quills straight into the hunters' behinds. Boog and Elliot squirted them with spray cheese, while the rabbits lured the hunters under the trees and into a trap.

"Fire!" called the Furry Tail Clan. They pelted the hunters with canned soup, toolboxes, coffeepots, and flashlights.

"Let's get out of here!" one hunter cried.

Reilly was buzzing away at a log bridge with his

"Ha, ha, ha!" cried Reilly, firing up his chain saw.

"Now let's kick some hunter behind!" Boog shouted as he and the animals pulled out silver shields, forming a protective silver barrier, and marched forward.

Meanwhile, Elliot, the deer herd, McSquizzy, and Mr. Weenie charged on the hunters from the other direction. The bucks lowered their antlers and stormed

chain saw. When the hunters tried to cross, they fell into the stream below, where they were slapped in the face and pummeled by Kung Fu Fighting salmon.

"Back to the trucks!" one of the hunters cried.

Elliot couldn't believe it—the hunters were on the run! "Boog, it's working!" he yelled excitedly.

But there was one hunter who wasn't about to give up.

"Hello, Goldilocks," Shaw said to a surprised Boog.

Gonk!

Elliot knocked Shaw's gun away before he could fire it.

Snarling, Boog attacked. But Shaw was tough. He grabbed Boog's nose and yanked. Elliot tried to help. He used a slingshot to fire a flashlight at Shaw.

But it hit Boog in the head instead. "Elliot!" Boog called. "Stop helping me!" But he managed to turn Shaw around so that he was in Elliot's line of fire.

Poof!

Shaw got hit with a pillow.

"A pillow?" Boog turned to Elliot. "Aw, come on, Elliot!"

"Okay, mama's bear, let's see what you got!" Shaw taunted, pulling out a knife. He swiped at Boog.

But Elliot used the slingshot to fire a golf club. Boog caught it and swung at Shaw. He knocked Shaw off his feet.

Shaw reached for his gun.

"Help me!" Elliot shouted to the other animals as he loaded himself into the giant slingshot. *Sproing!* Elliot flew through the air—and knocked Shaw's gun out of his hands.

Elliot crumpled to the ground in a heap.

When Boog saw Elliot, his best friend, lying on the ground, he suddenly got mad. He couldn't stand to see Shaw treat another animal like this. Boog realized that he was no longer a pet. He was now a wild grizzly bear.

Boog growled ferociously and lunged at Shaw, bending his gun around his arms and legs so that he couldn't move. Boog hurried over to help his friend.

"You all right, Elliot?" Boog asked.

"I'm a little light-headed," Elliot said. Then his one good antler cracked and fell off.

Boog laughed.

With a cheer, the animals rushed over to Shaw. They poured maple syrup over him and covered him in pillow feathers.

Boog helped Elliot to his feet. "You know, Elliot," he said as he looked around at the forest. "This place isn't so bad."

Suddenly, a helicopter landed nearby. The animals stopped what they were doing as Beth stepped out. "Boog?"

Boog ran to her and licked her face.

"What's he doing?" Reilly asked.

"She's his mom," Elliot explained. "She's taking us home."

"Every buddee?" the porcupine asked hopefully.

"Come on," Beth said to Boog, "let's go home."

Boog started to walk toward the helicopter, but stopped. He looked over at Elliot, then down in the dust. Dinkelman was lying at his feet. Boog picked up his teddy bear and walked after Beth.

Elliot's head dropped, his heart breaking. It looked

like he wasn't invited to live with Boog, after all. Then
Boog stopped in his tracks. Beth turned around to look
at him.

"Boog?" Beth said as the bear dropped Dinkelman
in her hands.

Boog looked back at the animals. Beth saw all the

animals watching Boog.

"Oh, you are home" Beth said. She understood that Boog wanted to stay with them.

"I'm so proud of you," Beth whispered as she hugged Boog.

Beth got back into the helicopter and flew away. Boog walked over to Elliot.

"She's coming back, right?" Elliot asked.

"Elliot, we're staying here," Boog said, pointing to the other animals. "This is our home, these are our people, this is where we reside." Boog leaned against a tree that Reilly had just knocked to the ground with his chain saw. Boog had come a long way from the garage. And while the forest didn't have a comfortable bed or delicious chocolate bars, it had his friends. And that was all he needed. The bear breathed in the fresh air and sighed happily. "Feels like home, baby," he said.

And it definitely did.